我有好朋友

文／孟瑛如
圖／蔡浩軒
英文翻譯／吳侑達

U0058223

　　恐龍王國裡住著一位自卑的暴龍王子，他總覺得自己因為長相凶惡，所以沒有朋友。他長了太多像牛排刀一樣鋒利的牙齒，只要一笑，他的大嘴就會咧到耳根後，那上下加起來五、六十顆往內彎、白森森的牙齒就會爆出來，看起來一副凶惡模樣！

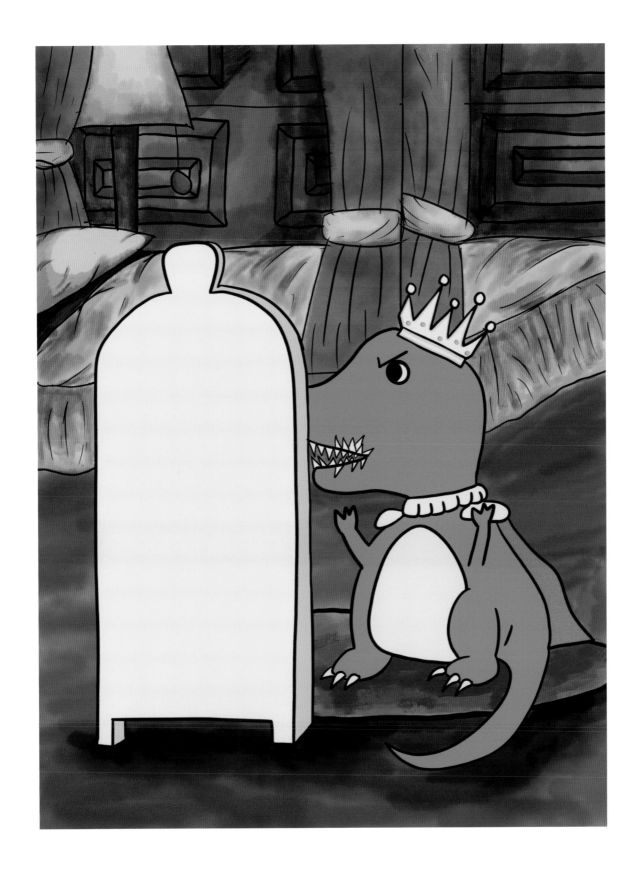

　　因此，暴龍王子總是看著鏡子練習閉緊嘴巴，盡可能不要笑。但這樣一來，他看起來就愈發嚴肅，也就愈發沒有任何動物敢接近他了！

　　有一天，當暴龍王子又寂寞的看著窗外時，突然發現河馬和許多動物一起在外面玩得不亦樂乎！休息時，河馬張大了嘴巴，還有牙籤鳥親熱的跑進他的嘴巴裡，幫他清除牙縫中的各種食物殘渣。大家看起來又愉快、又自在！

　　暴龍王子看到河馬張開 150 度的大嘴巴裡，只有長長的、突出的門齒和犬齒，還有四到六顆下門齒。他突然靈光一閃：「河馬的嘴巴跟我一樣，一笑就會咧到耳根後，但他卻這麼受歡迎、有這麼多朋友，而且笑容這麼可愛，一定是因為他的牙齒數量比較少！」

　　暴龍王子決定去找牙醫師，請他拔掉自己過多的牙齒，好讓自己的笑容可以跟河馬一樣迷人，這樣才可以交到許多朋友！

　　暴龍王子向王國裡最有名的牙醫師說明想法後，牙醫師就笑到樂不可支的說：「你有這麼多牙齒，應該是我們牙醫師的夢幻病人吧！不過，你的牙齒還不算多，鴨嘴龍的牙齒數目才驚人，有多達兩千多顆呢！他們還不是有很多朋友？而且也是我們牙醫師的好病人呢！」

　　牙醫師對著躺在診療椅上，幾乎要壓垮椅子的暴龍王子說：
「不要一直想著為什麼我都沒有朋友？而要想著我想跟誰做
朋友！」

　　暴龍王子絕望的說：「我一笑，大家就都跑掉了！我不笑，大家又說我嚴肅，也不敢靠近我！……我該怎麼辦呢？」

　　牙醫師看著快要哭出來的暴龍王子，笑得更厲害了：「交朋友又不是只靠笑容！交朋友，更不會是靠拔牙齒做出來的『扁』笑容！」

　　牙醫師忍住笑意繼續說：「想要交朋友，除了保持笑容外，是不是應該要知道對方的名字啊？」

　　暴龍王子說：「對喔！我不知道他們的名字，常常只叫對方『喂』或是綽號！」

　　牙醫師又說：「而且也要知道對方喜歡什麼話題，才可以聽他們說喜歡的事情，一起聊天啊！」

　　暴龍王子說：「啊！我常常只說我自己想說的，而且要別人一直聽我說！」

　　牙醫師接著說：「另外，也要知道對方喜歡做什麼事、玩什麼
遊戲，才可以一起做喜歡的事跟玩遊戲啊！」

　　暴龍王子的頭愈垂愈低：「以前，只要大家在一起的時候，我
常規定他們只能玩什麼或者只能做什麼事！」

牙醫師還說：「想要交朋友，一定要讓對方覺得他對你來說是很重要的！」

暴龍王子問：「但這要怎麼做呢？」

牙醫師說：「要常常考慮到對方的需求，或是誠心誠意的想讓對方開心啊！給予對方真誠適時的幫助，或者在重要時刻陪伴他，像是對方的生日是3月5日，你就可以在當天的3點5分發簡訊祝他生日快樂！酷吧？哈哈哈！」

牙醫師最後說：「還有，要讓朋友覺得跟你在一起可以很自在！」

暴龍王子又問：「什麼是自在呢？」

牙醫師回答：「找出你們的共同點，去做可以一起做的事，學會欣賞、包容和陪伴！」

　　回到城堡後，暴龍王子決定試試牙醫師的方法來交朋友。他開始認真記住大家的名字，沒多久，他就叫得出草原及森林裡大部分動物的名字了！許多動物都對暴龍王子叫得出自己的名字，感到又驚又喜，也開始願意靠近他了！

　　暴龍王子會試著在大家一起玩耍時，慢慢靠近看看大家都在玩
什麼？聊什麼？而不再像以前一樣躲在城堡裡自怨自艾，覺得大
家都不來邀他一起玩。現在暴龍王子自己走出城堡，看著大家快
樂的玩在一起，感覺其實也很好！

暴龍王子就這樣每天站著，每天接近一點點！

每天聽著，每天了解一點點！

每天接著別人的話題說，每天多聊一點點！

有時他也會給意見，尊重別人的想法，每天多給一點點！

　　慢慢的，暴龍王子了解到：兔子在一起時會討論要如何保養自己的毛皮，豬卻一定要去泥塘裡打滾，才能去除掉身上的寄生蟲——這其實也是一種保養毛皮的方式！

　　羊和牛要吃草，兔子在旁邊啃胡蘿蔔……他們也可以一起試試胡蘿蔔、蔬菜及青草的混合餐！也可以讓暴龍王子用鋒利的牛排刀牙齒切碎蕨類及植物幫大家加菜，大家都很開心！

雞和狗不一定要互相追逐，搞得雞飛狗跳，他們也是可以一起玩耍的！

　　就像湯姆貓跟傑利鼠天天見面，也不一定總要貓鼠大戰，他們可以花時間了解對方，好好和平共處，學會互助合作，獲取食物及歡樂的機會都更多！

　　想幫忙口渴的烏鴉喝瓶子裡的水，可以做根麥稈吸管給他！
想喝多少，就喝多少！

　　想幫忙聲音消失、無法表達的美人魚公主，可以告訴王子是美人魚公主從海邊救了他，或者讓美人魚公主寫紙條、傳 email 或 LINE 給王子！方法有很多！

　　龜兔賽跑的故事可以不再是老情節的傳統跑步競賽，而可以是合作競賽。烏龜和兔子可以一起出發，兔子扛著烏龜直到河邊，然後由烏龜接手，背著兔子過河。等到了河的對岸，兔子再扛著烏龜，兩個一起抵達終點！比起過去老情節的競賽活動，他們都感受到一種更大的成就感！

現在，暴龍王子終於明白牙醫師說的話了：

「不要一直想著為什麼我都沒有朋友？而要想著我想跟誰做朋友！」

5G時代已經到來，許多父母慣性的將 3C 產品塞給孩子，讓 3C 取代自己陪伴與教育的功能，殊不知適量的 3C 可以拉近孩子跟世界的距離，但過量的 3C，卻有可能切斷孩子對於世界的感覺！網路世界擾攘多變到讓我們不再需要人際互動，因為網路世界裡每天上演的都比真實世界中的人際互動更奇詭，每個網路世代的人都迫切要求時時自我更新最高版本，每個人都急著說而不想聽，急著寫而不想讀，急著展翅卻忘了籠寬。網路世界擾攘而擬真，真實世界卻相對沉寂而失焦。許多父母在各種親職教育的場合憂心忡忡的表示，擔心自己的孩子不會與人互動、在學校裡沒有朋友，這使我想到，或許我們不該一直針對孩子交不到朋友的負向現象去討論與悲嘆，而該聚焦在引導孩子如何交朋友的正向解決問題方法，也就是回到最原始、簡單的人性與群性。不一定需要很多的物質堆砌，最主要是被愛與被關心的感覺，會讓任何人覺得心靈富足！

因此，我想到用多數孩子很有興趣的恐龍和動物們來營造如何交朋友的故事，讓故事裡的牙醫師溫和堅持的用愛說實話，讓想交朋友卻用錯方式的暴龍王子好好思考，找出六種讓人喜歡他的方法：

- 付出真誠的關心
- 經常友善的微笑
- 叫出對方的名字
- 認真聽對方談他的事
- 跟對方談他喜歡的話題
- 讓對方覺得他對你很重要

引導孩子觀察暴龍王子如何慢慢建立友誼的過程，或許下次面臨類似問題時，我們可以好好鼓勵孩子：「不要一直想著為什麼我都沒有朋友？而要想著我想跟誰做朋友！」

I Have Many Good Friends!

Written by Ying-Ru Meng
Illustrated by Hao-Syuan Cai
Translated by Arik Wu

Once upon a time, there was a Dinosaur Kingdom. The prince, T-Rex, had always felt somehow inferior to other animals as he believed he looked horrible and had no friends. The reason why he thought so was because of his fifty or sixty dagger-like teeth. When he smiled, he would dramatically reveal every single one of these serrated, inwardly-facing teeth.

Prince T-Rex had always tried to practice in front of a mirror how to keep a straight face and keep his mouth shut at all times. He appeared more and more serious and unapproachable as a result, and even fewer animals would come near him.

One day when Prince T-Rex was looking out of the window, feeling quite lonely, he saw a hippo hanging out with a lot of other animals out there. When taking a short break in between activities, the hippo opened his mouth widely and allowed a plover to walk in there to remove decaying food lodged between his teeth. Everyone seemed at ease and was genuinely having a good time.

Prince T-Rex noticed that there were only several long, outstanding incisors and canines as well as four to six mandibular incisors in the hippo's mouth, and he suddenly came to realize why the hippo was so popular among animals. "Hippo has a mouth as big as I do and would dramatically expose every single one of his teeth when he smiles," Prince T-Rex thought to himself. "But he is so popular among animals, has so many friends, and has the loveliest smile ever — It has to be because he has fewer teeth than I do!"

Prince T-Rex then decided to have his redundant teeth removed by a dentist, so that he could have a smile as lovely and charming as the hippo and make many friends.

After hearing what Prince T-Rex had in mind, the most famous dentist in the kingdom burst into laughter. "You are the most ideal patient for us dentists as you have so many teeth. But well, hadrosaurids have even more teeth than you do. It's mind-blowing! They still have many friends though, and are also some of our most welcome patients!"

The dentist said to Prince T-Rex, who was so heavy that the therapeutic chair had almost been crushed, "Don't think about why you don't have many friends, think about whom you are going to be friends with."

"What should I do? Every time when I smile, they'll just go away!" Prince T-Rex said in despair. "But if I keep a straight face, they'll just say I look too serious to hang out with. What should I do?"

Looking at the teary-eyed prince, the dentist laughed even harder. "You can't make friends with smiles only," he said. "And you definitely can't make friends with a 'toothless' smile."

"If you want to make friends, you need to keep a smile on your face at all times," the dentist tried hard to refrain from laughing. "And shouldn't you remember their names?"

"Well," Prince T-Rex responded. "I always say 'hey' or simply call them by their nicknames, instead of actually remembering their real names."

"You also need to know some of the topics that interest them," the dentist said. "So you can get the conversation going."

"Got it! I think I talk about topics that only interest me way too often and not care what others have to say," Prince T-Rex said.

"You have to be aware of what they like to do and what games they like to play," the dentist continued. "So you all can get along well."

Prince T-Rex's head dropped in disappointment. "I used to boss around telling everyone what to do and what to play."

"If you want to make friends," the dentist said. "You need to make them feel important."

"How do I do that?" Prince T-Rex asked.

"Care for others often, and put your heart into making them happy," the dentist continued. "Also, you need to reach out to help them, or keep them accompany on important occasions. For example, if the birthday of your friend is on March 5th, you might want to send him a birthday message at 3:05 sharp on that day. Isn't that cool? Haha."

"Make sure your friends feel comfortable hanging out with you!" the dentist said.

"What does that mean?" Prince T-Rex seemed confused.

"It means you must find what you share in common, what you can do together, and learn to appreciate, tolerate, and how to stay by their sides when they are in need."

Prince T-Rex decided to give it a try when he returned to his castle. He started memorizing everyone's name and, in a short while, had remembered the names of almost all the animals living on plains and in forests! Many animals found it surprising and flattering that the prince actually took the effort to remember their names and started to feel closer to him.

Instead of staying in the castle complaining why no one wanted to invite him over, Prince T-Rex tried to approach other animals when they were hanging out, to see what they were doing and talking about. He actually felt quite happy about being able to walk out of his comfort zone and see other animals having fun together!

Little by little, step by step, Prince T-Rex tried to approach the animals a bit closer every day, to understand them a bit better, to chat with them a bit longer, and, sometimes, to give a bit of his own opinion without appearing offensive.

Prince T-Rex gradually came to realize that rabbits loved to talk about how to maintain their fur in perfect condition, and pigs needed to wallow in mud to remove ectoparasites to keep their skin in good condition.

He also realized that cows and sheep loved grazing on grass and rabbits would stay by their sides eating carrots. However, they would not mind eating a mix of carrots, vegetables, and grass either. Prince T-Rex even shredded pteridophytes and plants into pieces with his dagger-like teeth to complement their meals — everyone was very happy!

What also came to Prince T-Rex's realization was that dogs did not necessarily need to chase after chickens and cause disturbance everywhere — they could actually get along quite well!

Similarly, despite having to see each other every day, Tom and Jerry in the famous TV animated series actually do not need to waste their time fighting. Instead, they can spend more time getting to know each other and learning to get along and cooperate. That way, they will surely have way more food and happiness!

If a thirsty crow wants to drink water from a pitcher, we can make him a straw so he can drink as much as he wants!

If we want to help the poor, voiceless Little Mermaid tell the prince it was her who saved his life, we can have Little Mermaid write him notes, send him emails, or even message him on LINE! There are plenty of ways to help!

Likewise, instead of racing against each other, the tortoise and the hare can work together through the race. The hare can carry the tortoise to the river, have the tortoise take him to the other side of the river, and then carry the tortoise all the way to the end. That way, they will for sure achieve a bigger sense of achievement!